# MERRY ~~KRIS~~ CHRISTMAS MOM and DAD

## BY MERCER MAYER

A Random House PICTUREBACK® Book

**Random House** 🏠 **New York**

*Merry Christmas, Mom and Dad* book, characters, text, and images © 1982 Mercer Mayer. LITTLE CRITTER, MERCER MAYER'S LITTLE CRITTER, and MERCER MAYER'S LITTLE CRITTER and Logo are registered trademarks of Orchard House Licensing Company. All rights reserved. Published in the United States by Random House Children's Books, a division of Random House, Inc., New York. Originally published in 1982 by Golden Books Publishing Company, Inc. PICTUREBACK, RANDOM HOUSE, and the Random House colophon are registered trademarks of Random House, Inc.
www.randomhouse.com/kids
Educators and librarians, for a variety of teaching tools, visit us at
www.randomhouse.com/teachers
Library of Congress Control Number: 81-84377
ISBN-13: 978-0-307-11886-8    ISBN-10: 0-307-11886-X
Printed in the United States of America
25 24 23 22 21 20 19 18 17 16 15 14
First Random House Edition 2006

 wanted to make
Christmas very special
just for you,
so I made a Christmas wreath.

I wanted to decorate
some Christmas cookies
just for you,
but I couldn't stop
tasting them.

I wanted to find a Christmas present just for you,
but there were too many toys to look at.

So I asked Santa to bring you a special present instead.

I wanted to wrap
the baby's present
just for you,

but the tape was too sticky.

I picked out a Christmas tree
just for you...

but it was too big
to take home.

I wanted to carry
the Christmas balls
just for you,

but the box was upside down.

So I got out
the Christmas lights,
but they were
all tangled.

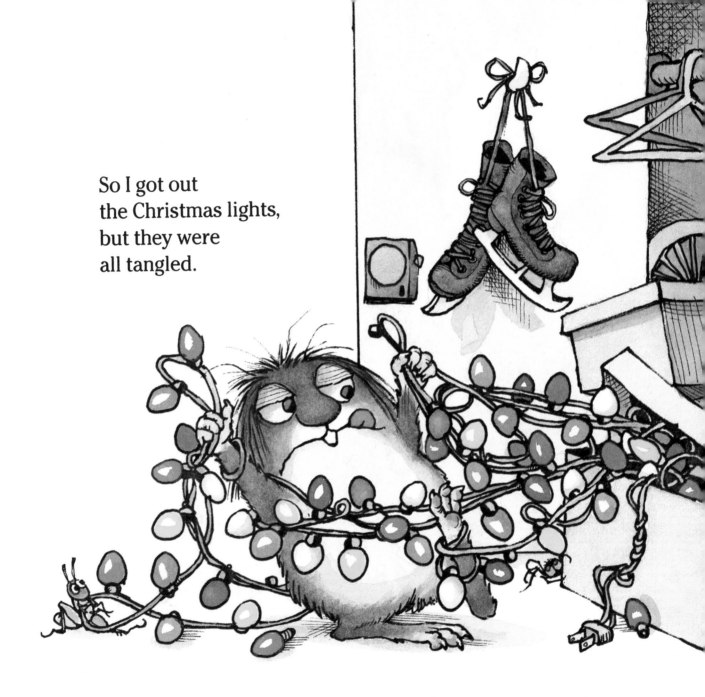

I wanted to put the star
on top of our tree
all by myself...so Dad helped.

On Christmas Eve
I tried to go right to sleep
just for you,

but I was too excited.

I didn't want to make you get up
too early on Christmas morning…

...so I brought my toys
upstairs to show you.